Cloud Eyes

Cloud

KATHRYN LASKY

Eyes

Illustrated by Barry Moser

HARCOURT BRACE & COMPANY

San Diego   New York   London

I am grateful to James Crumley for the inspiration
of the prologue to his novel *Dancing Bear*, and for his
enthusiasm for this new version of his tale.   — K. L.

Printed in Singapore

Lasky, Kathryn.
Cloud Eyes/written by Kathryn Lasky; illustrated by Barry
Moser. — 1st ed.
p.   cm.
Summary: A young Indian dreamer finds a way to keep the bears
from destroying the honeybees' hives and to bring the sweet taste
of honey back to his people.
ISBN 0-15-219168-2
[1. Bears — Fiction. 2. Bees — Fiction. 3. Honey — Fiction. 4. Indians
of North America — Fiction.]   I. Moser, Barry, ill.
II. Title.
PZ7.L3274Cl   1994
[Fic] — dc20   93-37805

First edition   A B C D E

ONCE, long ago, there was a place where there were more bears than people.

There were black bears and brown bears, cinnamon bears and grizzlies. The bears, greedy for honey, would go deep into the vast forests and strip the hives from the bee trees. The bees, angry at the greedy bears for tearing apart the hives and robbing them of honey, would sting the people, whose flesh was more tender than the tough, furry hides of the bears. The people

did not know what the bears had done to anger the bees, but they did know that their honey pots stood empty. And they were sad, for there was no sweetness in the lodges. Babies were born and grew into children who had never tasted the honeybees' sweet gold.

There was just one boy, almost a man, who could remember the taste of honey. They called him Cloud Eyes.

While other boys hunted or scraped hides or cured meat, Cloud Eyes read the sky. His gift of finding stories in the clouds was as important as the skills of making tools or stitching moccasins; he could see and understand what

other people could not. He could hear spirits and listen to the language of the animals. He could read the meaning in both the clouds of the sky and the clouds of smoke that rose from the sacred pipes. He was a dreamer.

Without ever climbing a mountain, a dreamer could reach the top and see the valley below. And standing on the flat of a desert, a dreamer could feel the roundness of the whole earth.

Cloud Eyes dreamed of many things, but most often his dreams were of things as simple as the clear taste of honey. He wished for a way to bring the sweetness back to the lodges.

One day, out in the woods, Cloud Eyes spotted a great cinnamon bear with two cubs and decided to follow them. The bears moved noisily through the woods, and Cloud Eyes traveled softly within the shadows and behind the screen of the noise. He watched the bears closely as they went deep into the forest to where the bee trees grew.

The bears were indeed greedy. The mother bear ripped open the bark of a bee tree with her sharp claws. The rough bear tongues licked the honeycombs dry. When the honey was gone, the bears left the honeycombs broken and the sap bleeding from great gashes in the bark.

So Cloud Eyes saw why the bees were angry and why there was no honey for the people. He took out his sacred pipe and, as the smoke curled around him, sang the songs of thanks for all of the earth's good things. And he wept for those things lost.

The smoke gathered into clouds, the dying trees seemed to melt away, and the forest turned to sky. Cloud Eyes began to dream, to read the shapes in the smoke. Within the growing cloud, bees swarmed, then became peaceful. They settled down and tried to make honey, but the trees were too weak to support the hives.

A low buzzing came to Cloud Eyes' ear. From a claw mark in a tree, Great-grandmother Bee flew. She was big and hairy and had huge, bulgy eyes so shiny black that Cloud Eyes could see the reflection of his face in them. When Great-grandmother Bee spoke, her voice like cracking rocks, Cloud Eyes trembled inside.

"Listen!" she rasped in his ear. "I will give you a vision, Cloud Eyes, for you know the ways of the bees. I will show you now the ways of the bears." With her hairy, pollen-covered legs, she danced the bear steps.

Cloud Eyes thanked Great-grandmother Bee and set out to follow the bear tracks and the claw marks. He walked through the forest, into a valley sprinkled with star flowers, over a ridge

where chokeberry grew, down a hillside fragrant with juniper, and across a meadow thick with camas roots. All along the way Cloud Eyes sang the songs of thanks for the star flowers, for the chokeberries, for the sweet juniper, for the chewy camas roots. He sang the songs of sadness for the honey, now vanished, and for the suffering trees.

In a clearing near a brook he found a sleeping grizzly, the honey still glistening on his muzzle and his breath still sweet. Cloud Eyes prayed to the bear's spirit for forgiveness and quickly plunged his knife into the bear.

Cloud Eyes skinned the hide from the dead grizzly and ate a piece of the heart, then some of

the liver for strength. He scraped the fat and softened the skin by rubbing it with the bear's intestines. For three days he bathed and fasted until his human smell disappeared. Then he rubbed himself with the bear's fat and slipped into the bear's skin, now as soft as a deerskin shirt.

Cloud Eyes crouched in the moonlight for a bit to get used to his new skin. Then he moved off on all fours; the earth was spongy beneath his claws and the moon silver on his back. He grunted and snuffled and made all the bear sounds that Great-grandmother Bee had whispered in his ear.

Soon he found the bears, and they came forward to greet their brother. Cloud Eyes began to dance the steps Great-grandmother Bee had taught him. The bears grunted among themselves. These steps were a little different from their own. Their brother must come from beyond the three peaks, from the place of the crazy bears. They would not dance with him.

The second night, Cloud Eyes danced the bear steps again. This night some cubs joined the dance, for young bears do not know or care what is crazy. They are not suspicious of a place so far away as the land beyond the three peaks. When the older bears saw their cubs dancing, they quieted, and some of them joined in.

On the third night all the bears danced with Cloud Eyes. They danced from the time the moon was at the edge of the world until it swung high above the tallest pine. They danced as the sky became chinked with stars, and until the last star faded into the gray dawn. Then the bears dropped to the ground, exhausted, and fell fast asleep.

While the bears slept, Cloud Eyes ran back to the people and told them what had happened. Together they followed the hairy-legged bees to a new grove of bee trees.

In their excitement, the people nearly forgot to sing the songs of thanks or to make the sacred smoke that calmed the bees. But Cloud Eyes reminded them. So they all sang

and the smoke rose thickly. The humming bees were pleased and filled their hives with honey.

Soon the sleep of the bears wore as thin as the dawn's light. Their muzzles twitched as they smelled the smoke; their ears were filled with the humming of the bees and the sweet songs of thanks. Their empty stomachs rumbled. When they awoke they lumbered off to search for new honey.

When they came to the bee trees, the bears found the people and the bees there together, surrounded by clouds of smoke. The bees were humming, and the people were reaching carefully into the hollows of the bee trees and taking just enough honey for their honey pots.

Cloud Eyes came toward the bears, but they did not recognize him, for he did not wear the bear skin and no longer smelled of bear fat. He smelled of smoke and honey, and he sang a song of forgiveness. He offered a taste of honey to each bear, and because he knew the bears' deep, rumbly voices could never sing the sweet songs, he began to dance with them between the trees. The dance seemed familiar to the bears, as if they had danced it in a faraway time and place, as if it were a dance from a dream. And then the bears became as calm and gentle as the bees.

So at last the sweetness returned. However, Cloud Eyes never ate the honey, but instead

always offered his to the bears. The bears were satisfied and no longer clawed at the trees; many of the trees grew strong again, and the bees had a place for their hives.

Cloud Eyes grew to be a very old man. After he died, the people honored his memory during the first moon of each summer by eating no honey. These were called the days of the bear dance, before the harvest of the honey, when the air was filled with sacred smoke and the songs of thanks stirred in the wind.

So every baby born came to know the taste of the honeybees' sweet gold, and the sweetness never again left the lodges.

The illustrations in this book were done in graphite on plate bristol.

The display type was set in Rustikalis Black
by Latent Lettering, New York, New York.

The text type was set in Trump Medieval
by Thompson Type, San Diego, California.

Printed and bound by Tien Wah Press, Singapore

Production supervision by Warren Wallerstein and Kent MacElwee

Designed by Barry Moser and Camilla Filancia